MORE ANIMAL FRIENDS 2

Adventures for Bedtime Reading

by

Granny Elizabeth Ann

with illustrations by RVW Jackson

For children age range 4 onwards

Contents

1. Sally and Matilda

One day Sally the spider is basking in the sun, sitting upon a stone in a field. Suddenly she is jumped upon by a cat. Luckily for Sally - she manages to crawl away from underneath the cat. Poor Sally is quite scarred and she feels like crying. As she runs away, she just escapes being eaten by a bird who watches her running through the grass. But she manages to crawl under a stone - glad to be safe again.

Just as Sally is sheltering, she sees Matilda the mouse resting under a leaf. She's sitting there, tears pouring down her face. Sally wonders what the matter is. If she approaches Matilda, maybe she will be attacked. However, Sally is a very kind spider, so she ventures forth from under the stone and approaches Matilda. She asks: 'What is the matter?'

Matilda tells her she has been chased by a cat.

Sally tells her not to cry and that she too was chased by a cat. 'But right now we are both safe!'

Matilda is not so sure that the field is a safe place - they can be seen by birds, chased by wild animals, eaten by snakes or caught by humans. We really need to find somewhere safe. Sally agrees. And together, the mouse and spider carry on through the field - by now they are firm friends. At the edge of the field they spy a building.

'Let's go inside,' says Sally.

The place seems deserted.

'Good idea!' says Matilda.

In they go. They spy a hole in the wall. Sally lends a hand - I should say a leg - to Matilda, who manages to crawl through the tiny space. Inside, they find an empty room.

'Look!' says Matilda, 'Crumbs on the floor.' And to add to her delight, a piece of cheese. 'You are so clever, Sally! This really is a safe place.'

And Sally is delighted, as she has found some dead flies on the window sill.

Soon they are full of food and feeling safe - but tired. They decide to look for somewhere to sleep for the night. Matilda notices a big bungy cushion and crawls underneath with Sally curled up beside her.

Just as they are sleeping, suddenly they are awakened by a loud whirring noise. Sally peers out as the lady with a Hoover zooms into view. The lady shrieks at the sight of Sally and even louder on seeing Matilda.

'Run, Matilda!' says Sally, as another cleaner comes to see what all the noise is about.

Our two friends escape into another room and hide behind a chest of drawers. Meanwhile the two cleaners finish their work and hastily go home. Peace at last! Matilda and Sally manage to sleep.

As they awake, they feel hungry and go in search of food. Much to their disgust, the crumbs and flies have all gone. As they are searching, they hear a hand bell ringing. Sally jumps on Matilda's back with fright - it's very loud for her little ears. Suddenly they hear voices and Matilda runs towards a cupboard with Sally on her back, clinging on tightly. They look with surprise as various children come into view pushing and shoving one another as they jostle for their seats in class. Once more, Sally's ears are affected as the teacher roars for silence.

Children stop talking and Sally stamps her feet with approval as silence descends on the classroom. Our friends are safe under the cupboard - they can see out but nobody seems to notice them.

Trouble is, both feel very hungry. Then, a little girl at the back of the class stuffs a piece of cheese into her mouth, dropping a couple of crumbs. Matilda looks longingly at the cheese. Sally tells her to wait until the children go away. Matilda doesn't listen and darts out to get the cheese. The little girl screams and jumps on her desk. There's commotion in the class. Poor Sally tries to cover her ears with two of her eight legs. Matilda joins her and tells Sally they'd better find a way out before the cupboard is moved and they are found. Luckily for Sally and Matilda there is a hole in the wall. They squeeze through just as Teacher seems to be moving the chest. The hole leads to a pipe and Matilda and Sally find themselves sliding down - at quite a speed. They end up in a cellar for storing food. Matilda finds more cheese. But just as she is about to take a bite, a huge rat appears and tells her this is his home - and to buzz off! Matilda doesn't like the look of the rat and tells Sally it's time to go and find somewhere to live. The rat watches as the two friends flee through an open door which leads outside.

Soon Matilda and Sally are back near the field after dodging past traffic on the road. But they decide not to chance going on the field again.

Sally sees a funny building. 'Let's look inside,' he says.

'What on Earth is it?' says Matilda.

Our two friends had never seen a building like this one. Can we guess what it is? Yes, it's a windmill.

As they watch, the sails go round and round.

'Come on, the door looks open,' says Sally.

'Let's go round the back,' says Matilda, 'where we won't be seen.'

Sure enough, round the back they notice a hole in the base of the windmill. They crawl inside and see people walking around, one of them explaining how flour is made. They remain well hidden behind a stack of crates. The sounds of the man's voice and the rumbling machinery soon send them to sleep. An hour later all seems quiet, so they creep out into the mill. Sally clmbs up a bag of flour and tries eating some. Matilda laughs as Sally is covered in the stuff.

'Urgh! That tastes awful!' says Sally.

'I agree,' says Matilda.

But they gaze in wonder at the structure of the windmill which had been grinding the flour.

'Be careful. Sally,' Matilda says. Although it was now quiet, they had watched earlier and seen how the flour was produced and Matilda didn't want Sally to get hurt.

As the two friends look around the windmill, they see a smaller room made into a kitchen. Somebody has left a cupboard door open. Sally runs into the cupboard and to her delight finds an open packet of biscuits.

'Look what I've found!' she calls to Matilda, who pushes hard with her foot and sends the packet onto the floor below. This breaks several biscuits and the two friends enjoy a good feast. Sally also finds a couple of dead flies to eat and Matilda finds a piece of cheese. They decide it's best to leave now as they can hear someone coming towards the mill. They first manage to find the hole to get back outside and then hear a man's voice shouting to his mate: 'Someone's broken the biscuits! If it's mice or rats, we'd better get rid of them.'

Matilda decides it is time to move on. They hurry across the field, away from the windmill and arrive at a wood. They look around for some food and manage to find an old sandwich and a piece of cake. Sally finds a dead fly and a beetle. After their meal it is time to think about somewhere to stay.

'I'll crawl up this tree and have a look around,' Sally says. She finds an empty nest and calls for Matilda to join her. Matilda finds it hard work climbing the tree and says she will stay there for the night but look for a new place tomorrow.

That night, the friends don't sleep very well. The owls keep them awake and then it starts to rain. Matilda feels cold and wet. She pulls at some leaves for shelter and their nest rocks in the wind and rain.

'Be careful or we'll both fall out!' warns Sally. Next morning they hurry down the tree and search for food again.

The rain had left plenty of puddles, so at least they can have a drink. But lots of flying insects are around and food is in short supply.

After breakfast they continue walking and find that the wood is quite small. They are back on the road again but staying hidden by the hedges.

They soon notice a house where a group of unruly children are being bundled into a car by their mum. Matilda sees an open window.

'They are in a hurry,' says Matilda. 'Let's have a look and see what's inside! It's a kitchen window and the place could be in a mess.'

The car drives off and the two friends climb through the open window. Inside, the breakfast things haven't been cleared away and they find plenty of food scraps on the floor.

They soon decide to look upstairs and see several bedrooms - also very untidy - with one bedroom floor covered in biscuit crumbs.

'Let's have a rest under the bed,' says Sally, 'before we go outside again.'

Just as they are falling asleep, they hear the front door open. Someone comes in. It's the children's mother, who begins to clean up the kitchen and put the cereals away, lastly cleaning the floor. She then makes herself a cup of coffee and goes into the living room. Matilda and Sally hear them moving around downstairs and wonder if it is safe under the bed. Then Sally notices a hole in the skirting board just big enough for Matilda. They both squeeze through and agree it would be OK to live behind this hole, which they explore and find that it leads to the inside of the garage roof - plenty of room and safe for hiding!

For the next few days the friends only come out when the children have left for school. Each day they have plenty to eat in the kitchen and usually find half drunken cups of orange juice. Sometimes the taps may be left running in the kitchen or bathroom. The friends decide to settle in this house and stay, at least for a while...

****

2. Felix the Hungry Fox

Felix was quite a small fox but he wanted to go out into the world and leave his family behind.

One night he ran away from his hillside home and the safety of his den and family. As he ran across the hills, he noticed a road and made for it. As it was night time, it was deserted. So Felix happily jogged along - until a huge lorry passed by. He realised this was quite a scary place to be! So he kept near the edge of the road. Next, he met up with a hedgehog. Felix tried to feel it and of course yelped in pain as the spikes hurt his paw.

'Buzz off!' shouted the hedgehog.

Felix quickly ran off. But next, he saw a snake that hissed at him.

'Dear me!' complained Felix. 'These creatures aren't very friendly.'

Then he met a hare who told him to go back home to his family. But Felix carried on. Finally he reached a wood and decided to go inside. By now he was tired. He bedded down under some leaves and fell fast asleep.

Next morning, Felix felt very hungry but it was difficult to find any food. Eventually he did find something. Yes! A half eaten sandwich. Just as he reached for it, down flew a crow who snatched it away and flew off.

Nearby was a piece of meat, but once again a bird was quicker than Felix and again he couldn't reach the food in time. Felix began to get upset and wished he hadn't left home.

Suddenly, a red squirrel appeared and asked him why he was crying. Felix told him he was very hungry and nobody would share their food with him.

The red squirrel, being very kind, said, 'Look, you can hide behind this big tree because soon the forest rangers will be putting out food for the red squirrels. I'll share some with you.'

Sure enough, the rangers brought some nuts and the little squirrel called Sammy gave some to Felix. It wasn't what Felix had ever eaten before and it took quite a lot of chewing, but he quite enjoyed the nuts.

The two friends played hide and seek together and also played catch with a half eaten nut. Then they lay in the wood for a rest.

Sammy said to Felix, 'Soon some human day-trippers will be coming, many bringing nuts. I'll go up to them, collect the nuts and bury them until we need more food.'

Felix watched from behind the tree as Sammy ran up to people who were just behind a wire fence. As people threw nuts over the fence, Sammy was joined by more squirrels who collected them, some eating them on the spot and others burying them in the forest for later. Felix decided he would help and ran to where the nuts were being thrown. The people behind the fence were surprised and shouted out, which made the other squirrels all disappear, many running up the trees. But Sammy continued to collect the nuts. This happened again for two more days until Felix heard a man complaining and saying the fox needs to go.

By now, Felix was tired of eating only nuts and he was missing his Mum, Dad and family.

He told Sammy, 'I'm worried about the man who said I had to go. And I'm really missing my home even though I've enjoyed your company.'

'That's OK,' Sammy said, 'I've worked out where you live and instead of going back along the road, I can show you a short cut through the woods. Let's wait until dark and then I will go with you.'

The friends played together and when night came they set off for Felix's home. This was a very quick route and Felix soon saw the hillside where his den was located.

Mummy fox was looking out and shouted for joy when she saw Felix. Felix explained where he had been and how Sammy had helped him. Mummy fox hugged Sammy and invited him into the den to have a meal with the family.

Mummy and Daddy fox then told Sammy he was welcome to visit whenever he wanted and Felix would be allowed to play with him. This pleased the two friends and Felix waved to Sammy who then set off for his home in the forest.

*****

3. Heidi Hedgehog

Heidi was quite a small hedgehog and had been the last in the litter. Today was exciting, as her Mum and Dad had decided that she could now go out on her own. But she had been given strict instructions to be back by nightfall. If she met anyone who might hurt her, Mum told her to roll herself into a ball and keep her paws tucked up. Also, to make sure that her face didn't get injured.

Heidi started off at quite a fast pace and soon left her home behind. She was thrilled to see all the birds flying about.

Suddenly, she was confronted by a large dog who barked at her. Remembering her mother's advice, she quickly rolled herself into a ball. She felt a push as the dog tried to see where her face had gone. Then she heard the yelp as Heidi's spikes caught the dog's paw. The dog decided this creature wasn't very friendly and he ran off, along with his mistress. Heidi waited until all was quiet and peeped out.

'Nobody around!' she murmured, as she started walking towards the woods.

After walking for a long time she felt tired, so she had a rest in some leaves. Again, she rolled herself into a ball and this time fell asleep. Suddenly a group of children came into the wood, collecting leaves for a nature table. A little boy picked up some leaves and caught his hand on Heidi's spikes.

The teacher in charge decided the llittle boy's hand was OK and cleaned it up. While she was busy, Heidi ran off and hid under another pile of leaves. She found herself next to an injured bird who was in pain.

'Can I help?' asked Heidi.

'Yes, please - I'm hungry and thirsty,' the bird replied.

Heidi, being kind, went looking for some food. She managed to find an old apple core thrown away by one of the children. The bird - a jackdaw called Bertie - was gratefull and pecked at the apple core and was also pleased with the remains of some juice in an opened plasic bottle which Heidi rolled towards him.

'You're in luck!' said Heidi. 'This was left by a naughty child who should have taken it home. And there's more. We can share this half eaten cheese sandwich.'

But just as she was rolling the empty bottle out of the way, her paw was caught on some barbed wire, from which she couldn't escape.

Bertie saw what had happened and tweeted loudly. This was heard by a little girl.

'Over here, Daddy!' she called to her father, who was a vet. 'Can you help this bird?'

'OK Janet!' The vet came over and tried to pull Bertie up, but the bird squeaked a lot and was distressed at the thought of leaving his new found friend. But he calmed down when he saw that Janet was also aware of the hedgehog and his badly hurt paw.

Janet and her Dad picked up the two injured friends and put them in an animal enclosure box in the back of the vet's car. The two friends were rather worried:

'I can smell cats!' whispered Bertie.

'It's OK, said Heidi. 'There are none in here and at least we're together.'

On reaching the vetinary surgery, the box was taken inside and the vet looked first at Heidi's paw. He cleaned it up, gave her an injection for any pain and then sewed up the wound. Next, he put her in a safe place.

'Now it's your turn,' the vet said, carrying Bertie to the table, where he looked at the bird's wing. 'If I put a splint on it, this should be much better in a few days.'

Bertie made it plain that he wasn't going to be separated from his friend, so the vet decided to leave them together.

Soon, the two friends were both feeling much better. The vet and Janet watched Bertie helping helping Heidi to eat some food. They were quite amazed at this friendship, and over the next few days both animals improved and slept close to each other.

'Daddy,' suggested Janet, 'When these patients are better, we should return them to the wood.'

This they did.

Bertie was now able to fly, but continued to stay at Heidi's side.

'I'd better return home, Bertie!' said Heidi. 'My parents will be worried. Thank you for friendship and I'll miss you.'

'Yes!' said Bertie, 'We can look out for each other and perhaps meet up again.'

Heidi set off, as she had much to tell of her adventures in the wood and at the vet's surgery.

*****

4. Gemma and Bengy

Gemma was a lovely grey rabbit who lived with a little girl called Susie. She liked where she lived and loved to play with Susie - and missed her when she went to school. Gradually, Gemma gave up running into the garden and spent all day in her hutch. And Susie was worried about her.

Sally's mum said, 'I think we need to buy another rabbit to keep her company.'

So Susie and her mum set off to town to look at two rabbits that were for sale. These two rabbits were called Bengy and Mike.

Bengy was a small, white and ginger rabbit who had seven brothers and sisters. These were all white rabbits. They made fun of Bengy and weren't very kind to him.

They belonged to Jane who had four rabbits. When they were born, she decided that they would have to go to diffrent homes.

The first family came to look at them and picked a large white rabbit. Several other families came and each time a white rabbit was chosen - until they were down to Mike and Bengy.

'Nobody will want you,' Mike told Bengy, 'I expect to go next!'

Then along came Susie. She looked at Mike Rabbit and then at Bengy, who was hiding in a corner of the hutch. She scooped up Bengy and stroked him gently.

'You're beautiful!' she said. 'Please can I have him, Mummy?'

Bengy was thrilled because he liked Susie and she gently carried him to the car. When they reached Susie's home, Bengy was taken into the garden where a lovely hutch was ready for him with a catflap, allowing him to go into a fenced off garden area. Susie put him in the hutch where a grey rabbit called Gemma was resting. Bengy was afraid and curled up into a ball.

'Don't be afraid, little one,' said Gemma, 'I'm so glad you have come to keep me company - I was so lonely on my own.'

Bengy was so surprised: 'But don't you think I'm ugly with my brown patches?'

'Not at all!' said Gemma. 'I think they make you look handsome.'

Bengy ran towards the grey rabbit and sat near her. He told her about his brothers and sisters.

'Well, I'm glad you came,' she said,' I was lonely on my own. Susie is very kind and did play with me when I was little. She does come and give me a cuddle when she gets home from school. But during the day I sit in the hutch or run into the garden area.'

Gemma showed Bengy how to use the catflap and they both ran into the garden. Susie and her mother watched as the two rabbits ran around.

'See,' said Susie's Mum, 'Gemma just needed some company!'

The two rabbits became great friends and played in the garden most of the day. Both looked forward to Susie coming home, when she unlatched the hutch and let them run free around the garden and gave them both a cuddle. Gemma was so happy to have a friend and Bengy loved his new home and Gemma, his new friend.

*****

5. Reggie Robin

Reggie Robin lived in quite a big garden with a big tree in the middle. He had left his home and was now ready to live alone and hoped to find a lady robin.

The first problem was that he was quite small and the crows and pigeons were very greedy and seemed always to get first to any food thrown into the garden.

Help was at hand because the lady of the house noticed Reggie struggling to get food. So she bought a bird table with a second platform and put plenty of birdseed on the bottom layer. The pigeons were too big to get to this layer. Reggie was delighted at being able to reach this birdseed. This annoyed the pigeons and that night they plotted to chase poor Reggie from the garden.

Reggie was asleep when he felt someone trying to knock him off his perch in the tree. Two pigeons were by his nest and soon Reggie found himself falling towards the grass. Just in time he managed to flap his wings and fly higher so that he did not hit the ground. However, he did hurt his wing and for a few days he hid in the long grass to recover.

The lady of the house was surprised not to see Reggie hopping around and she hoped he was still OK. After three days Reggie came out of his hiding place and went to the bird table. To his delight he found some birdseed, fresh water and some fat balls. But suddenly the pigeons came flying into the garden and once again tried to attack Reggie. However, the lady of the house chsed them off with a yard brush and told Reggie she was really pleased he was back.

For the next few days Reggie followed the lady around when she was in the garden, especially if she did any gardening and turned over the soil, treating Reggie to worms.

Reggie was happy but he felt lonely without a partner. One day, he was really scared when a huge white bird came into the garden. To Reggie he looked like a monster. This bird was a seagull and he told Reggie he was very hungry, as he hadn't been able to find any food. Reggie tipped some of the seed from the bird table onto the ground along with some bread he found on the upper platform. The seagull was very grateful and Reggie also showed him where to find fresh water.

Then the pigeons returned to the garden and stopped in surprise when they saw the seagull called Ray, who told them he was making this garden his land-based home.

'And if you try to attack Reggie again,' Ray said, 'you'll have me to deal with!'

So the pigeons flew far, far away...

Meanwhile, Reggie lived in the garden quite happily. One day another robin flew into the garden. Reggie was delighted to find she was a lady robin called Vicky. The two robins got on very well and Reggie invited Vicky to stay with him in the big tree which was his home. Soon they built a nest and Reggie was so proud when his son was born. Ray the seagull still came to visit, but the pigeons never came back.

*****

the

end

Printed in Poland
by Amazon Fulfillment
Poland Sp. z o.o., Wrocław

64155265R00021